D1556163

Harry
and the Muddy Pig

By Ruth Chesney

Illustrated by Mary Weatherup

JOHN RITCHIE LTD
CHRISTIAN PUBLICATIONS

40 Beansburn, Kilmarnock, Scotland

ISBN-13: 978 1 910513 74 3

Copyright © 2017 by John Ritchie Ltd.
40 Beansburn, Kilmarnock, Scotland

www.ritchiechristianmedia.co.uk

Typeset by John Ritchie Ltd., Kilmarnock
Printed by Bell & Bain Ltd., Glasgow

This is Harry.

Harry lives on a farm with Daddy, Mummy, Little Sister Susie and Toby the dog.

It was the day before the Show and Gladys the pig was very
muddy. She couldn't go to the Show like that!

So Daddy and Harry washed Gladys the pig. First they hosed her down…

…then they scrubbed her with soapy bubbles. Toby the dog chased the bubbles and ate them!

They rinsed Gladys with buckets of water. Harry threw water over Daddy by mistake! Oops!

Next they dried Gladys with a fluffy towel…

…and put her into a clean pen with some fresh sawdust.

Next morning, Daddy and Harry ate boiled eggs and toast for breakfast.

"It's the Show today," said Daddy. "Let's go and put Gladys into the trailer."

Daddy and Harry went to the shed…

…but Gladys was gone! "Oh no!" cried Daddy.

Harry peeked into the other pens, but Gladys wasn't anywhere to be found.

Then he heard a noise coming from behind the shed.

'Grunt!'   'Grunt!'   'Grunt!'

They ran to see…

…and there was Gladys, happily rolling in the biggest, muddiest mud puddle you've ever seen!

"Oh, Gladys!" groaned Daddy.

So Daddy and Harry waded into the mud puddle to fetch Gladys...but she didn't want to get out.

They poked her and prodded her and pushed her.

Finally Gladys got up and slowly strolled to the yard. "Hurry up, Gladys!" said Harry.

Then they washed Gladys again, only faster this time! They hosed her…and scrubbed her…and rinsed her…and dried her…

…and put her straight into the trailer. Harry made sure the trailer door was properly closed!

Mummy came outside with Little Sister Susie. "What ha[...]ened?" she asked. "You both look like you've been rolling in m[...] You'd better change your clothes before the Show!"

Daddy and Harry changed their clothes.

They all set off for the Show, with Gladys safely in the trailer.

"Daddy," said Harry, "why did Gladys the pig want to go back to the mud after she was all nice and clean?"

Daddy laughed. "Harry, that's because she's a pig and that's what pigs do!" he answered. "There's a verse in the Bible that talks about a pig who was washed going back to rolling in the mud."

(2nd Peter 2:22)

"Is there?" asked Harry.

"Yes!" said Daddy. "And we are all like Gladys, except it isn't mud that we want to go back to. Instead it's all the bad things we do. These bad things are called sins."

"Like telling lies and being cheeky and not doing what we're told?" asked Harry.

"Yes, those are sins," said Daddy. "And just like Gladys goes back to the mud because she is a pig, so we keep going back and doing sins because we are sinners."

"But the Lord Jesus died on the cross to take away our sins. We can't change ourselves, but when we trust in Him He changes us and helps us not to do those bad things anymore."

"There's another verse in the Bible, which says, 'If anyone is in Christ, he is a new creation; old things have passed away; behold, all things have become new.' God is the only One Who can change us."

(2nd Corinthians 5:7)

"But Gladys will always be a pig!" said Harry.

"That's right," agreed Daddy.

Harry cheered when Gladys the pig came first in her class and won a bright red rosette.

Then they went for a walk around the Show and saw shiny tractors, furry rabbits, home-grown carrots and gigantic bulls.

Harry ate a hot dog and nearly half a bag of candyfloss…

…and had a ride in an aeroplane.

Then it was time to go. Little Sister Susie was getting sleepy.

And when they got home, guess where Gladys went?

The mud puddle!

Grunt!